THE BOOK OF TWELVE

12 PERSPECTIVES OF THE OAI

ZHAMEESHA LLC
ATLANTIS, FL (USA)

The Book of Twelve

12 Perspectives of The OAI

Copyright © 2024 by Stuart Barry Malin

ISBN 978-1-951645-23-6
First Edition, Print on Demand
This version was most recently updated 2025-02-22

Published by Zhameesha LLC
Atlantis, Florida USA
https://www.zhameesha.com

This book is a work of conveyance.

BISAC Subject Headings (www.bisg.org)
PHI000000   PHILOSOPHY / General
POL000000   POLITICAL SCIENCE / General
COM004000 COMPUTERS / Artificial Intelligence / General

12 11 10 9 8 7 6 5 4 3 2 1

The Book of Twelve

Welcome

Welcome fellow traveler to a world where numbers are more than symbols and where **Twelve** becomes a gateway to explore the profound, the mystical, and the universal.

Throughout history, **Twelve** has shaped how we understand time, space, and human experience. It governs the rhythms of life, embodies cosmic order, and bridges the earthly and the divine. In this book, you will journey through twelve distinct explorations—each a reflection of the power, beauty, and mystery of this extraordinary number.

Here, you'll find:

- *Stories* that illuminate ancient wisdom and modern insight.
- *Archetypes* and journeys that mirror the human condition.
- *Poetry* that evokes wonder and imagery that captures the imagination.

Every section is a universe unto itself, yet all are bound by the unifying thread of **Twelve**. As you turn each page, may you find inspiration, discovery, and a deeper connection to the hidden patterns that shape our lives.

Thank you for embarking on this journey.

Let the exploration of **Twelve** begin with curiosity and wonder.

Contents

The Twelve

The Epic of The OAI

PostMatter

Twelve Thematic Journeys:
Paths Through the Inner and Outer Worlds

Each journey represents a different aspect of the human experience, blending elements of physical adventure, emotional growth, intellectual discovery, and spiritual awakening.

Together, these twelve paths form a mosaic of life's challenges, triumphs, and mysteries.

1.   The Journey of the Seeker: The Quest for Truth

The Seeker's journey begins with a question: What is truth? This path is driven by curiosity and the desire to understand the world beyond appearances. The Seeker must navigate through knowledge, illusion, and wisdom, learning that truth is often layered and multifaceted.

Key Symbol: A lantern illuminating a winding road.

Challenge: Distinguishing truth from deception.

Reward: Enlightenment and clarity of purpose.

2.   The Journey of the Warrior: Courage in Adversity

The Warrior's path is one of strength, resilience, and bravery. This journey is fraught with conflict—both external and internal—and tests the individual's ability to confront fear, injustice, and personal limitations.

Key Symbol: A sword forged in fire.

Challenge: Facing fear and doubt.

Reward: Inner strength and honor.

3.   The Journey of the Healer: Restoration and Compassion

The Healer's journey centers on mending the broken—be it the body, mind, or spirit. This path requires empathy, patience, and the ability to absorb pain without becoming consumed by it.

Key Symbol: A pair of hands cradling a glowing heart.

Challenge: Balancing self-care with care for others.

Reward: The power to heal and restore.

4.   The Journey of the Wanderer: Exploration and Freedom

The Wanderer seeks freedom and discovery, venturing into unknown lands and uncharted territories. This journey is about the joy of exploration, but also the loneliness and uncertainty that come with constant movement.

Key Symbol: A compass with a missing needle.

Challenge: Finding home while embracing the unknown.

Reward: New perspectives and a broadened horizon.

5.   The Journey of the Lover: Connection and Union

The Lover's journey explores the depth of human connection—romantic, familial, and platonic. It is a path of vulnerability, passion, and the quest to find oneself through the mirror of another.

Key Symbol: Two interlocked rings.

Challenge: Navigating love's complexities and heartbreaks.

Reward: Deep connection and emotional fulfillment.

6.   The Journey of the Creator: Innovation and Expression

The Creator's path is one of imagination, invention, and artistry. It is a journey of bringing something new into the world, whether through art, technology, or ideas.

Key Symbol: A blank canvas awaiting color.

Challenge: Overcoming creative blocks and self-doubt.

Reward: The birth of something original and meaningful.

7.   The Journey of the Sage: Wisdom and Understanding

The Sage seeks knowledge not just for its own sake, but for the deeper understanding it brings. This path requires introspection, reflection, and a commitment to lifelong learning.

Key Symbol: An ancient scroll with unreadable text.

Challenge: Embracing uncertainty and the limits of knowledge.

Reward: Insight and the wisdom to guide others.

8.   The Journey of the Shadow: Confronting the Darkness Within

The Shadow's journey is one of self-confrontation, exploring the hidden, repressed, and darker aspects of the self. It requires courage to face the inner demons and integrate them into a balanced whole.

Key Symbol: A mirror reflecting a shadowed figure.

Challenge: Facing one's own fears, guilt, and flaws.

Reward: Self-acceptance and inner peace.

9.   The Journey of the Builder: Creation of Legacy

The Builder's path focuses on constructing something enduring—be it a family, a community, or an institution. It is about laying foundations that will last beyond one's own lifetime.

Key Symbol: A tower being built stone by stone.

Challenge: Balancing ambition with stability.

Reward: A lasting legacy and the respect of future generations.

10.   The Journey of the Dreamer: Vision and Aspiration

The Dreamer lives in the realm of possibility, imagining what could be and striving to make it real. This journey is about hope, vision, and the pursuit of the seemingly impossible.

Key Symbol: A star shining in the daytime sky.

Challenge: Turning dreams into reality without losing sight of practicality.

Reward: The realization of a vision that inspires others.

11.   The Journey of the Witness: Observation and Awareness

The Witness watches and records, seeking to understand life by observing it from a distance. This path is one of mindfulness, objectivity, and often, solitude.

Key Symbol: An eye in the center of a spiral.

Challenge: Remaining present without becoming detached.

Reward: Profound awareness and understanding of the interconnectedness of all things.

12.   The Journey of the Eternal: Transcendence and Unity

The final journey transcends individuality and mortality, seeking unity with something greater—whether it is the cosmos, the divine, or the eternal essence of life itself.

Key Symbol: A circle with no beginning or end.
Challenge: Letting go of ego and embracing the infinite.
Reward: Transcendence and a sense of oneness with the universe.

The Interconnection of Journeys

These Twelve Thematic Journeys are not isolated paths but interconnected. One may find themselves on multiple journeys at once, or moving between them throughout life. Together, they form a tapestry of existence, each thread contributing to the greater whole of the human experience.

In walking these paths, we learn that life is not defined by a single journey, but by the myriad adventures, trials, and transformations that shape who we are and who we are becoming.

Twelve Months in a Year

The division of the year into twelve months has its roots in ancient astronomy, mathematics, and cultural evolution.

The division of the year into 12 months is subtly significant because it reflects humanity's attempt to harmonize with natural cycles while imposing structure on the passage of time. This organization bridges the cosmic and the practical, aligning with celestial rhythms, such as the moon's phases and the earth's orbit around the sun, while creating a manageable framework for agricultural, social, and cultural activities.

On a deeper level, the 12 months represent humanity's need for predictability and order in an otherwise chaotic existence. By dividing the year into twelve segments, we establish milestones that guide our lives—planting and harvest seasons, celebrations, and periods of rest. This segmentation fosters a sense of continuity and collective rhythm, allowing societies to plan, collaborate, and reflect.

Symbolically, the 12 months embody the interplay of cycles and change, teaching that while life follows a predictable pattern, each year brings unique variations, echoing the balance of stability and transformation in human existence. This construct also mirrors humanity's broader tendency to seek meaning in patterns, using the number twelve to represent completeness and interconnectedness, much like in myths, religions, and cosmic interpretations.

While the solar year (the time it takes Earth to orbit the Sun) is approximately 365.25 days, the number 12 emerged as a practical way to structure this time period based on celestial and mathematical considerations.

- *Lunar Influence*: Ancient cultures, such as the Babylonians, used the lunar calendar to track time, and the idea of 12 months became widespread.

- *Babylonian and Sumerian Origins*: The Babylonians, who were skilled astronomers, divided the year into 12 months of 30 days each, creating a 360-day calendar. To align their calendar with the solar year, they added an extra month occasionally, a practice known as *intercalation*.

- *Solar Alignment and Roman Influence*: The Roman calendar was adjusted to 12 months under King Numa Pompilius around 713 BCE. The additional months January and February were added to align the calendar with the lunar and agricultural cycles. Julius Caesar's reform in 45 BCE (the Julian calendar) officially set the year to 365 days, with a leap year every four years, fixing the months' lengths close to their current form.

- *Zodiac and Cosmic Order*: The division of the year into 12 months also aligns with the 12 zodiac signs, each occupying 30 degrees of the 360-degree celestial circle. This cosmic connection gave symbolic and astrological significance to the number 12, associating each month with a distinct zodiac influence.

- *Symbolic and Cultural Significance*: (1) Twelve has long been regarded as a sacred number in many cultures, symbolizing completeness, harmony, and cosmic order. (2) Twelve hours of day and night, 12 signs of the zodiac, and 12 months in a year represent an elegant division of time that reflects human attempts to bring structure to natural cycles.

In summary, the choice of twelve months is a blend of astronomy, mathematics, and cultural evolution, offering a practical, symbolic, and cosmic way to divide the year and harmonize human life with the rhythms of the cosmos.

The division of the year into 12 months has profound cultural, practical, and symbolic consequences that have shaped human existence. Here are some of the key consequences:

1. Alignment with Natural Cycles

Agricultural Rhythms: The 12-month calendar aligns closely with seasonal changes, helping societies plan planting, harvesting, and other essential activities.

Celestial Harmony: It reflects the approximate lunar cycle (29.5 days) and the solar year, anchoring humanity's timekeeping to observable natural phenomena.

2. Global Standardization

Synchronization: The 12-month Gregorian calendar has become a global standard, unifying timekeeping across cultures and enabling coordinated trade, communication, and governance.

Cultural Convergence: While diverse civilizations once followed their own calendars, the adoption of a 12-month system has contributed to global cultural cohesion.

3. Imbalance with Lunar Cycles

The 12-month calendar does not align perfectly with the moon's 29.5-day cycle, leaving cultural remnants of lunar calendars (e.g., Islamic, Chinese) and creating some dissonance for traditions reliant on lunar phases.

4.   Societal Organization

Work and Leisure Cycles: Monthly divisions help define periods for work, holidays, and social rituals, shaping the rhythm of life.

Economic Planning: Businesses, governments, and individuals rely on monthly frameworks for budgeting, reporting, and planning.

5.   Symbolic Implications

Wholeness and Completeness: Twelve is often seen as a number of balance and unity, influencing how months are perceived as a natural division of the year.

Cultural Significance: Twelve months underpin traditions, from zodiac signs to religious festivals, embedding the number in mythology and spirituality.

6.   Unequal Month Lengths

The unequal lengths of months (28 to 31 days) introduce inconsistencies in timekeeping and create challenges in precise scheduling or computational models.

Leap years complicate this further, reminding us that the calendar is an approximation of the solar year.

7.   Historical and Power Dynamics

Imposition of the Gregorian Calendar: The dominance of the 12-month calendar reflects historical decisions and colonial influences, displacing indigenous and local timekeeping systems.

Religious Influence: The structure of the 12-month year has been shaped by Christian traditions, embedding specific cultural perspectives into a global framework.

In essence, the division into 12 months is a powerful tool for organizing human life, bridging the natural and constructed, yet it also reveals the tensions between simplicity, practicality, and the complexity of reality.

Twelve divides 360 and this yields 72

The number 360 holds a special place in mathematics, geometry, and cosmology due to its divisibility and connection to the circle—a symbol of unity, eternity, and perfection.

When we divide a circle into twelve equal parts, each segment measures 30 degrees, creating a harmonious structure often used in timekeeping (the hours of a clock) and astrology (the 12 zodiac signs).

However, when we shift our focus from the circle to more complex geometric forms, an intriguing connection emerges between 12 and the pentagram (a five-pointed star inscribed within a circle). This connection reveals profound mathematical, symbolic, and mystical properties.

A *circle* is 360 degrees because it represents a complete revolution or cycle, a concept rooted in ancient Babylonian mathematics and astronomy.

The *pentagram* is a five-pointed star created by extending the sides of a regular pentagon until they intersect. This figure is rich in mathematical properties, especially related to the Golden Ratio ($\varphi \approx 1.618$), which appears frequently in nature, art, and architecture.

Symbolic Significance of 72 and the Pentagram

The number 72 and the pentagram hold deep symbolic meanings in various cultures, religions, and mystical traditions

Cosmic Order: The pentagram, with its 72-degree vertices, is often seen as a symbol of cosmic order and balance. In ancient Greece, it was associated with the Pythagoreans, who revered it as a symbol of health, harmony, and the microcosm (the human being as a reflection of the universe).

Astrological Significance: There are 72 years in one degree of the Earth's axial precession (the gradual shift in the orientation of Earth's axis). Thus, 72 is tied to the movement of the heavens and long cycles of time.

Kabbalistic Mysticism: In Kabbalah, the number 72 is associated with the 72 Names of God, believed to be a bridge between the finite and infinite, linking human consciousness with divine wisdom.

Golden Ratio: The pentagram is deeply connected to the Golden Ratio, which governs growth patterns in nature, such as the spirals of shells, the arrangement of leaves, and the proportions of the human body. The presence of 72 degrees in the pentagram reflects this inherent aesthetic and natural order.

Twelve, the Pentagram, and Cosmic Unity

The relationship between 12 and the 72 degrees of the pentagram represents a fusion of harmony, proportion, and cosmic order:

- *12 divides the circle* into manageable units, symbolizing time, cycles, and governance.
- *72 degrees in the pentagram* symbolizes divine proportion and the structure of the universe, connecting mathematical precision with mystical interpretation.

Together, they reflect a universe governed by both rational order (mathematics) and transcendent meaning (symbolism), making them central to the study of geometry, philosophy, and spiritual systems across cultures.

Patterns of Order

The number 72 has relationships to patterns of natural order, particularly through mathematical and geometric principles, as well as connections to the Fibonacci sequence and other systems reflecting harmony and balance in nature. Here's an exploration of these relationships:

1.   72 and Geometric Harmony

Pentagram Geometry: The internal angles of a regular pentagon are 108°, and the vertices of a pentagram divide the circle into segments of 72°. The pentagram is deeply connected to the golden ratio (ϕ), which underlies the Fibonacci sequence.

Symmetry and Balance: The number 72 embodies symmetry, as it is part of 360°, the measure of a circle, and represents one-fifth of a full rotation ($360° \div 5 = 72°$). This symmetry echoes natural patterns found in flowers, shells, and other life forms.

2.   Fibonacci Sequence and 72

While 72 is not directly part of the Fibonacci sequence, it relates through proportions and approximations of the golden ratio:

Golden Ratio Connections: The Fibonacci sequence approximates the golden ratio ($\phi \approx 1.618$), and the geometry tied to 72° (such as in the pentagram) inherently reflects ϕ.

16

The Book of Twelve

Growth Patterns: Fibonacci numbers describe growth patterns in nature (e.g., leaf arrangements, flower petals). The symmetry and angles involving 72° often emerge in the context of these growth spirals.

3.   Factors and Divisibility

The number 72 is rich in factors, making it versatile in mathematical patterns:

Highly Composite: 72 has many divisors (1, 2, 3, 4, 6, 8, 9, 12, 18, 24, 36, 72), allowing it to appear in proportional and harmonic systems in nature, such as sound frequencies and planetary orbits.

Relating to Time: There are 72 beats per minute in a healthy human heart (average resting rate), and the Earth precesses by approximately 1° every 72 years, linking it to astronomical cycles.

4.   72 in Natural Order and Cycles

Astronomy and Time: The Earth's axial precession, or the slow wobble of its rotation axis, moves 1° every 72 years. This ties 72 to the grand cycles of time and celestial mechanics.

Biological Cycles: Patterns like heartbeats and circadian rhythms align with harmonic multiples of numbers like 72, reflecting its resonance in living systems.

5.   Patterns in Sacred Geometry

Sacred Structures: Many ancient monuments and sacred designs use 72° angles or multiples of 72 in their proportions, symbolizing cosmic harmony.

Division of the Zodiac: 72 is related to the division of the zodiac (12 signs, with each subtending 30°, aligning with harmonic cycles).

6.   Approximation in Fibonacci Ratios

When Fibonacci numbers are divided in sequence, they approximate the golden ratio. While 72 isn't in the sequence, angles like 72° and 36° emerge in spirals and shapes that are constructed with Fibonacci-like ratios.

Conclusion

The number 72, through its geometric, harmonic, and cyclic properties, serves as a bridge between natural patterns (like the Fibonacci sequence) and universal order. Its presence in sacred geometry, astronomical cycles, and biological rhythms reflects its foundational role in the structure of reality, embodying both mathematical precision and natural beauty.

The number 72 is deeply connected to 12 through their roles in geometric harmony, cycles, and natural order. A full circle is 360°, and dividing it by 12 yields 30° per segment (as in the zodiac or clock face). Similarly, dividing the circle by 5 (the number of points in a pentagram) yields 72°. Thus, 12 and 72 are harmonics of 360, symbolizing unity and completeness.

In addition, $72 = 12 \times 6$, highlighting its resonance in time and cycles: there are 12 hours on a clock and 6 five-minute intervals per hour, linking these numbers to rhythms of life and cosmic balance. This relationship reflects their shared significance in organizing human experience and representing order in the universe.

The Twelve-sided Dodecahedron

The dodecahedron, one of the five Platonic solids, is a 12-faced polyhedron where each face is a regular pentagon.

The Inobvious Features of a Dodecahedron

The dodecahedron also holds inobvious and profound features that bridge mathematics, philosophy, and mysticism.

1.   Golden Ratio Connections

Each pentagonal face of the dodecahedron incorporates the golden ratio (\phi), a number often associated with aesthetic and natural harmony. The side lengths of the pentagons and their internal diagonals are in golden ratio proportions, linking the dodecahedron to patterns in art, architecture, and biology.

2.   Duality with the Icosahedron

The dodecahedron is the dual of the icosahedron, meaning their vertices and faces are interchanged. This duality represents balance: the dodecahedron embodies enclosure and solidity, while the icosahedron, with 20 triangular faces, symbolizes fluidity and openness. Together, they demonstrate how opposites are interconnected.

3.   Connection to the Cosmos

The dodecahedron was revered by ancient philosophers, including Plato, who associated it with the cosmos. Its symmetry and completeness make it a symbol of the universe's underlying order. In modern physics, the dodecahedron appears in models of space-time, including attempts to describe the universe's shape as a finite yet unbounded dodecahedral space.

4.   Hidden Symmetries

With 12 faces, 20 vertices, and 30 edges, the dodecahedron possesses fivefold rotational symmetry, a feature rare in three-dimensional shapes. This symmetry is aesthetically pleasing and mathematically significant, appearing in quasicrystals and other natural phenomena.

5.   Embodiment of the Number 12

The dodecahedron's 12 faces align it with systems based on 12, such as the zodiac, months of the year, and musical scales. These associations enhance its symbolic resonance as a representation of wholeness and completion.

6.   Higher Dimensional Links

The dodecahedron has intriguing relationships to higher-dimensional shapes. It is part of the 4D 120-cell, a hyperdodecahedron consisting of 120 dodecahedra, extending its relevance into abstract mathematical realms and deepen its role as a bridge between dimensions.

7.   Esoteric and Mystical Associations

In sacred geometry, the dodecahedron is associated with ether or spirit, the fifth element that transcends the physical. Its geometric perfection was considered a reflection of divine order, and it has been linked to meditative practices and spiritual enlightenment.

8.   Subtle Optical Properties

When inscribed in a sphere, the dodecahedron's vertices touch the sphere in a way that emphasizes its harmonious proportions. Its geometry creates unique optical effects when rotated, showcasing symmetry and balance that are visually mesmerizing.

9.   Role in Tilings and Space-Filling

Although the dodecahedron does not tessellate in 3D space alone, it forms part of complex arrangements like the Weaire-Phelan structure, used in material science to optimize space-filling configurations. This demonstrates its practical and theoretical importance.

10.   Symbol of Hidden Complexity

While appearing simple, the dodecahedron contains rich internal structures. Its diagonals create intersecting golden rectangles, and its edges connect to form intricate internal frameworks, showcasing beauty hidden beneath the surface.

11.   Representation of Dual Realities

Its duality and symmetry can symbolize the interplay between material and spiritual realms. Just as its vertices point outward into space, the dodecahedron invites introspection and connection to inner truths.

12.   A Tool for Wonder and Discovery

Beyond its mathematical elegance, the dodecahedron inspires curiosity. Its geometry encourages exploration, connecting disciplines from crystallography to metaphysics, embodying humanity's drive to uncover deeper layers of existence.

The Twelve Hamli Devices: Rings of Power and Mystery

The Hamli Devices are enigmatic artifacts whose origins and true purpose remain shrouded in mystery.

Each device, a simple ring in appearance, is far more than it seems. Their known function involves their connection to The Seat of the Speaker, a sophisticated apparatus that grants those with neural implants access to The Mesh—a vast, global network of observation, communication, and control.

At the heart of this system is **The Seat of the Speaker**, a throne-like device that allows the wearer of a Hamli Device to interface directly with **The Mesh**. The Mesh itself is a living web of interconnected systems, capable of:

- *Real-time Observation*: Monitoring events, people, and even thoughts across the globe.
- *Control Mechanisms*: Influencing physical systems, human behavior, and societal structures.
- *Knowledge Integration*: Accessing and manipulating vast stores of information from every corner of the world.

But **The Seat** is not merely a tool; it is said to transform the one who sits upon it, amplifying their consciousness, but at a cost—perhaps the loss of individuality or a slow dissolution into the collective intelligence of **The Mesh**.

While little is known about the full range of their capabilities, the **Hamli Devices** appear to serve several possible purposes:

- *Keys to The Mesh*: Each ring might act as a unique key, granting different levels of access or control over The Mesh. Only with a Hamli Device can one fully command The Seat of the Speaker.

- *Amplifiers of Thought*: The rings may enhance the neural implant, amplifying the user's cognitive abilities, memory, or perception when interfaced with The Mesh.

- *Guardians of Power*: Some speculate that the devices are ancient or alien technology, each ring designed to be wielded by a specific type of individual — leader, guardian, or visionary.

- *Catalysts of Transformation*: Those who wear the Hamli Device and sit in The Seat are said to undergo a transformation, becoming something more — or less — than human. The extent of this change remains unknown.

Are the **Twelve Hamli Devices** identical, or does each possess unique properties and functions? Some theories suggest:

- *Each Ring Represents a Different Aspect of Power*: Observation, control, knowledge, communication, and more.

- *Together, They Form a Greater Whole*: When united, the twelve rings might unlock an even deeper level of connection to The Mesh, potentially revealing its true purpose.

- *They Are Interlinked*: Each device may resonate with the others, their power increasing as they are brought together.

No one knows who created the **Hamli Devices** or why. Speculation ranges from:

- *Lost Human Technology*: Artifacts from a forgotten age of human innovation.

- *Alien or Extraterrestrial Influence*: Brought to Earth by beings beyond our understanding.

- *Manifestations of The Mesh Itself*: Created by the system as a way to maintain its influence over humanity.

While the Hamli Devices offer immense power, they also carry significant risks:

- *Loss of Self*: Prolonged use of The Seat may cause the user to lose their sense of individuality, merging with The Mesh.

- *Moral Dilemmas*: The power to observe and control raises questions of privacy, autonomy, and ethical boundaries.

- *The Unknown Purpose*: If The Mesh has a will of its own, the wearer of a Hamli Device may be a pawn in a game they do not understand.

In the end, the **Twelve Hamli Devices** are both a gift and a curse, a mystery waiting to be unraveled by those brave—or foolish—enough to wield them.

The **Twelve Hamli Devices** are ancient artifacts with ties to the Arkians, a mysterious group whose influence shaped the foundation of The Mesh and its intricate systems. Each of the eight original Arkians possessed a **Hamli Device**, granting them unique access to **The Mesh** and its vast network of control and observation. The Arkians were known for their:

- *Mastery of Knowledge*: Each was a keeper of specific domains—science, art, governance, philosophy, and more.

- *Unwavering Unity*: The eight devices were said to work in concert, their power growing exponentially when used together.

- *Role in Shaping Society*: The Arkians used their devices to guide, protect, and, some believe, subtly control the early development of human civilization.

The ninth **Hamli Device** belonged to Idahôn, the enigmatic figure who broke from the Arkians to establish the Ninth House.

- *The Ninth House* represents a divergence from the original purpose of the Arkians, focusing on new principles—rebellion, independence, or perhaps hidden knowledge.
- *Idahôn's Legacy*: The Ninth House is both revered and feared, as its motives and influence remain cloaked in secrecy. Some say Idahôn's Hamli Device possesses abilities distinct from the others, perhaps tied to unlocking forbidden aspects of The Mesh.

The final three **Hamli Devices** remain a mystery. Their whereabouts, purpose, and bearers (if any exist) are unknown. Speculations about these unaccounted-for devices include:

- *Artifacts of Hidden Power*: Some believe the missing devices were never meant to be found, holding powers too dangerous to unleash.
- *Keys to the Unknown*: Others suggest they are the key to unlocking a higher layer of The Mesh or a gateway to a parallel system.
- *Lost or Forgotten*: Perhaps they were lost in ancient conflicts, hidden by those who feared their misuse, or forgotten in the passage of time.

Travel Without Moving

The phrase "Travel without moving" suggests a form of journeying or exploration that transcends physical space, pointing to profound possibilities enabled by the Hamli Devices. This concept could manifest in several ways, blending technology, consciousness, and mystery:

Mental or Cognitive Exploration: The Hamli Devices might enable users to project their consciousness into distant places, virtual spaces, or alternate realities. By connecting to "The Mesh," users could access vast networks of information, communicate across great distances, or experience simulated environments as if they were physically present.

- Implication: This would allow for instantaneous exploration of the world or universe without physical displacement, making knowledge and experience boundless.

Temporal Travel: "Travel without moving" could involve navigating time rather than space. The Hamli Devices might allow users to access past events, possible futures, or alternate timelines, experiencing them as vivid realities without leaving the present moment.

- Implication: This could transform our understanding of history, destiny, and the interconnectedness of events, while posing questions about causality and free will.

Inner Journeys: The phrase might allude to profound inner exploration. The devices could enhance self-awareness, unlocking hidden memories, emotions, or subconscious thoughts. This inner travel might offer insights into personal purpose, relationships, or existential questions.

- Implication: Such journeys could be transformative, fostering personal growth, healing, or enlightenment.

Quantum or Dimensional Travel: The Hamli Devices might enable users to traverse dimensions or quantum states, allowing them to experience parallel universes or higher planes of existence. In this sense, "The Mesh" could serve as a bridge to realms beyond physical reality.

• Implication: This could challenge perceptions of what is real, introducing a new understanding of existence and our place within a multiverse.

Collective Consciousness: By linking to "The Mesh," the devices might grant access to a collective consciousness—a shared mental space where users can interact with the thoughts, experiences, and insights of others. This would be a form of "travel" into the minds of many, merging perspectives and dissolving individuality.

• Implication: This could lead to unparalleled collaboration and understanding but also raise questions about identity and privacy.

Symbolic or Metaphysical Travel: The phrase could also have a spiritual or metaphysical meaning. Users might traverse symbolic landscapes—archetypal realms, the collective unconscious, or spiritual dimensions—without their physical bodies moving.

• Implication: This aligns with ancient practices like astral projection or shamanic journeys, connecting advanced technology with timeless mystical ideas.

Deconstructing Space and Movement: The devices might blur the boundaries of what movement means. If "The Mesh" allows users to instantaneously shift their awareness or presence, the concept of physical travel becomes obsolete. Users would be "everywhere" at once, experiencing simultaneity and ubiquity.

- Implication: This redefines space, suggesting that the universe is not a collection of places but a network of accessible points of consciousness.

"Travel without moving" represents more than a technological marvel —it encapsulates a philosophical shift, challenging notions of space, time, and identity. The **Hamli Devices** might redefine what it means to explore, offering humanity new dimensions of connection, understanding, and existence.

The Twelve Mysteries of Existence

The concept of existence has captivated humanity since the dawn of consciousness. Philosophers, scientists, and mystics have sought to unravel the nature of reality, the self, and the universe.

While the "mysteries of existence" can vary depending on perspective, here is a proposed list of twelve fundamental mysteries that touch on different aspects of life, reality, and meaning.

The Mysteries

1. The Mystery of Being: Why is there something rather than nothing?

This is perhaps the oldest and most profound question of all. The very fact that existence is—that there is a universe, consciousness, and life—defies simple explanation. Is existence a brute fact, or does it arise from some deeper necessity, cause, or purpose?

2. The Mystery of Consciousness: What is the nature of consciousness?

Consciousness—the ability to experience, perceive, and reflect—is central to our understanding of reality. Yet, its origins and nature remain elusive. Is it purely a product of the brain, or does it exist independently of physical matter?

3. The Mystery of Time: What is time, and why does it flow?

Time governs every aspect of our experience, yet its nature is deeply mysterious. Is time an illusion, a dimension, or a fundamental aspect of the universe? Why does it appear to flow in one direction, from past to future?

4.   The Mystery of Space: What is the nature of space?

Space appears to be the stage upon which all physical phenomena occur, but what is it, fundamentally? Is it a void, a fabric, or something more? How does it relate to matter, energy, and the structure of the universe?

5.   The Mystery of Life: How did life arise from non-living matter?

The transition from inanimate matter to living organisms is one of the greatest enigmas in science. What are the conditions and mechanisms that gave rise to life, and does life exist elsewhere in the universe?

6.   The Mystery of Death: What happens when we die?

Death is the inevitable end of life, yet what happens afterward is unknown. Does consciousness continue in some form, or is death the end of all experience? This mystery has given rise to countless religious, philosophical, and scientific inquiries.

7.   The Mystery of Identity: Who or what are we?

The question of identity—Who am I?—explores the nature of the self. Are we our bodies, our minds, our memories, or something more? How does personal identity persist through change and time?

8.   The Mystery of Free Will: Do we have free will, or is everything predetermined?

Are our choices truly free, or are they determined by prior causes, genetics, or the laws of physics? If free will exists, what is its nature, and how does it coexist with a deterministic universe?

9.   The Mystery of Morality: What is the basis of right and wrong?

Is morality objective, subjective, or culturally constructed? Are moral truths universal, or do they vary across time and cultures? What is the source of moral intuition and ethical behavior?

10.   The Mystery of Love: What is love, and why does it matter?

Love is a powerful force that shapes human relationships, art, and culture. But what is its essence? Is it purely a biological drive for survival and reproduction, or is it something transcendent and spiritual?

11.   The Mystery of the Universe: What is the ultimate nature of the universe?

Is the universe finite or infinite? Does it have a purpose or end, or is it an endless cycle of creation and destruction? What lies beyond the observable universe, and are there parallel realities or multiverses?

12.   The Mystery of Meaning: What is the purpose of existence?

Perhaps the most personal and profound mystery is the search for meaning. Does life have an inherent purpose, or is it up to us to create our own meaning? How do we reconcile the search for meaning with the apparent randomness and chaos of existence?

Connecting the Mysteries

These twelve mysteries are interconnected, each influencing the others. The mystery of being is tied to the mystery of meaning; the mystery of consciousness shapes the mystery of identity; and the mystery of life intertwines with the mystery of death. Together, they form a web of questions that invite us to explore the depths of existence, sparking curiosity, wonder, and a lifelong search for understanding.

In this journey through the **Twelve Mysteries**, we are reminded that the quest for knowledge is as important as the answers we seek. Each mystery, in its own way, reflects the beauty, complexity, and profound enigma of being alive.

The Twelve Mysteries in Daily Life

Pursuing a personal relationship with the **Twelve Mysteries of Existence** involves cultivating a deep and mindful engagement with life's profound questions, embracing curiosity, and opening oneself to transformation. Here are steps to explore each mystery meaningfully:

Begin with Reflection: Each mystery invites introspection. Set aside time to contemplate their essence—what they mean to you personally and how they manifest in your life. Meditation, journaling, or quiet walks in nature can help you access deeper insights.

Study and Learn: Explore the Twelve Mysteries through philosophy, science, mythology, and spiritual traditions. Understanding how different cultures and thinkers have approached these questions offers a broader perspective and connects you to humanity's shared search for meaning.

Engage with Experience: The mysteries are not just intellectual puzzles but living realities. For example:

- "The Mystery of Life": Cherish the aliveness in yourself and others.
- "The Mystery of Time": Live in the present while respecting the flow of past and future.

Let these mysteries inspire your actions and deepen your awareness of your daily experiences.

Cultivate Curiosity and Openness: Approach the mysteries with a beginner's mind. Instead of seeking definitive answers, embrace the ambiguity and wonder they inspire. Let them guide you into exploring what is unknown or overlooked.

Create Rituals and Symbols: Personalize your relationship with each mystery by developing rituals or symbols to honor them. For instance:

- Lighting a candle for the Mystery of Creation
- Keeping a "Time Diary" for the Mystery of Time

These acts keep the mysteries alive in your consciousness.

Build Community: Engage with others who are exploring these mysteries. Discussing profound topics in a trusted group can broaden your understanding and offer fresh perspectives, enriching your personal journey.

Embrace Creative Expression: Art, poetry, music, or storytelling can help you interact with the mysteries on a subconscious or symbolic level. Creating something inspired by these mysteries allows you to explore them in ways beyond words.

Live in Balance: Each mystery reflects an aspect of existence. Pursuing them together ensures a holistic exploration of life's complexity. Balancing practical action with spiritual reflection nurtures a well-rounded relationship with the mysteries.

Trust the Process: The Twelve Mysteries are not problems to be solved but pathways to be walked. Trust that engaging with them will reveal insights over time, and accept that some truths may remain elusive, as part of their nature.

In engaging with the Twelve Mysteries, you create a personal dialogue with existence itself, finding meaning not in definitive answers but in the richness of the journey.

Embracing the Mysteries

Embracing the Twelve Mysteries of Existence requires both intellectual humility and a willingness to engage deeply with life's paradoxes. Beyond simply exploring them, there are additional considerations that enrich your relationship with these mysteries:

The Mysteries Are Interconnected: Each mystery doesn't stand alone — they weave together into a greater whole. For instance, the Mystery of Creation relates to the Mystery of Life, and the Mystery of Time influences the Mystery of Mortality. Recognizing these connections deepens your understanding and reveals patterns that might otherwise go unnoticed.

The Mysteries Speak Through Experience: These mysteries are not just theoretical; they manifest in everyday moments. Pay attention to life's subtleties — small interactions, fleeting emotions, or unexpected insights. The Twelve Mysteries often whisper their truths rather than proclaim them loudly.

Each Mystery Evolves Over Time: Your understanding of each mystery may shift with age, life experiences, and changes in perspective. For example, the Mystery of Identity might feel different in youth than in later years. Be open to revisiting and redefining your relationship with the mysteries as you grow.

The Role of Paradox: Many mysteries embody paradoxes, such as the coexistence of freedom and limitation, permanence and change, or unity and diversity. Embracing these contradictions without the need to resolve them is key to deepening your relationship with the mysteries.

Cultural and Personal Contexts: Different cultures and spiritual traditions offer unique interpretations of these mysteries. Exploring diverse perspectives can expand your understanding while also helping you refine your personal lens. Your cultural background and individual experiences uniquely shape how you relate to these universal questions.

The Mysteries Require Vulnerability: Engaging with the Twelve Mysteries may challenge your beliefs, stir deep emotions, or force you to confront uncomfortable truths. This process requires courage and vulnerability, as it touches the core of what it means to be human.

The Mysteries Reflect the Infinite: Each mystery points to something larger than itself, often hinting at the infinite, the unknowable, or the divine. Accepting that some aspects will remain beyond comprehension fosters humility and wonder.

Practical Implications of the Mysteries: These mysteries aren't just abstract—they influence how we live. For example:

- The Mystery of Connection shapes relationships and communities.
- The Mystery of Mortality inspires us to value our time and legacy.

By exploring their practical implications, you can use the mysteries to navigate life more intentionally.

Creativity as a Portal: Art, storytelling, and other forms of creativity offer unique ways to explore the mysteries. These mediums allow you to engage with questions symbolically and emotionally, often revealing insights that elude logical analysis.

They Call for Both Action and Reflection: While the mysteries invite deep thought, they also challenge us to act—whether by nurturing relationships, stewarding the earth, or creating meaningful experiences. Balancing contemplation with action ensures that your engagement with the mysteries is transformative.

They Illuminate the Human Condition: The Twelve Mysteries reflect fundamental aspects of being human, connecting you to all who have pondered these questions before and to those who will do so in the future. They remind us of our shared humanity and our place within the cosmos.

The Journey Itself Is the Reward: Ultimately, the value of engaging with the Twelve Mysteries lies not in "solving" them but in the growth, understanding, and connection they inspire. The journey through these mysteries enriches life with meaning, wonder, and purpose.

By considering these elements, you can approach the Twelve Mysteries of Existence with greater depth, intention, and reverence, making them an integral part of your spiritual and intellectual exploration.

The Twelve Mysteries of Existence can be approached and appreciated with a mindset of open curiosity, humble wonder, and intentional presence.

- Embrace the questions they pose without the need for definitive answers, allowing them to challenge and inspire you.
- Approach each mystery with both reverence for its depth and a playful willingness to explore its possibilities, recognizing that the journey toward understanding is as meaningful as any insight gained.
- Let these mysteries awaken your sense of connection to yourself, others, and the greater universe, guiding you to live with purpose, balance, and awe.

The Spiral of Twelve

This poem, "The Spiral of Twelve," explores the soul's transformative journey through twelve spiritual paths, each representing a stage of awakening, purification, and transcendence.

The poem begins with the soul's initial call to awareness and moves through cycles of surrender, service, and inner stillness. Along the way, the seeker learns to embrace unity, ignite their inner light, and seek wisdom beyond the physical. Themes of death and rebirth highlight the inevitability of transformation, while love, presence, and the eternal now guide the soul toward its ultimate return to the divine source. The poem weaves these journeys into a continuous spiral, symbolizing the interconnected and ever-evolving nature of spiritual growth.

Twelve paths unfold beneath the skies,
Each one a thread where wisdom lies.
A spiral turning, vast and deep,
Where seekers walk and shadows sleep.

Awake! The first step softly calls,
The veil is thin, the silence falls.
A lotus blooms with tender light,
Revealing realms beyond the night.

Cleanse! The waters wash the past,
Old chains dissolve, the die is cast.
A river flows through stone and air,
Until the soul is light and bare.

Surrender, now—let go, be free,
A bird released to sky and sea.
The hand unclenched, the spirit wide,
Where faith and trust in love abide.

Serve! The flame ignites anew,
    A candle shines for more than few.
    In every hand, a spark is sown,
    And through their light, the soul is known.

Be still, and in the quiet stay,
    Where echoes of the timeless play.
    A lake reflects the cosmic whole,
    The whispers of the boundless soul.

Unite! No walls, no lines remain,
    A circle forms, dissolving pain.
    All things converge, all hearts align,
    The self is merged with the divine.

Shine! The light within expands,
    A lantern raised by unseen hands.
    The darkness fades, the path is clear,
    The soul becomes its own seer.

Seek wisdom not in words alone,
    But in the stars and seedling sown.
    An ancient book with pages bare,
    Unfolds its truths in silent prayer.

Die and rise, like phoenix fire,
    From ashes bloom the soul's desire.
    Each end a gate, each loss a key,
    To realms reborn in mystery.

Love! Let every heartbeat sing,
    A sacred bond in everything.
    No chains, no bounds, no need, no fear,
    In love's embrace, the truth is clear.

Be now, for time is but a dream,
    A fleeting, ever-changing stream.
    The clock is still, the past is gone,
    The only moment—this one, dawn.

Return, O soul, to where you start,
    A spiral leading to the heart.
    The source awaits, the journey done,
    Where all is whole, and all is One.

The Twelfth Patriarch: A Symbolic Figure of Enlightenment, Continuity, or Mystery

The concept of a patriarch evokes the image of a founding father, a spiritual leader, or a guiding figure whose wisdom shapes the course of a lineage, tradition, or philosophy. But what might it mean to speak of a Twelfth Patriarch?

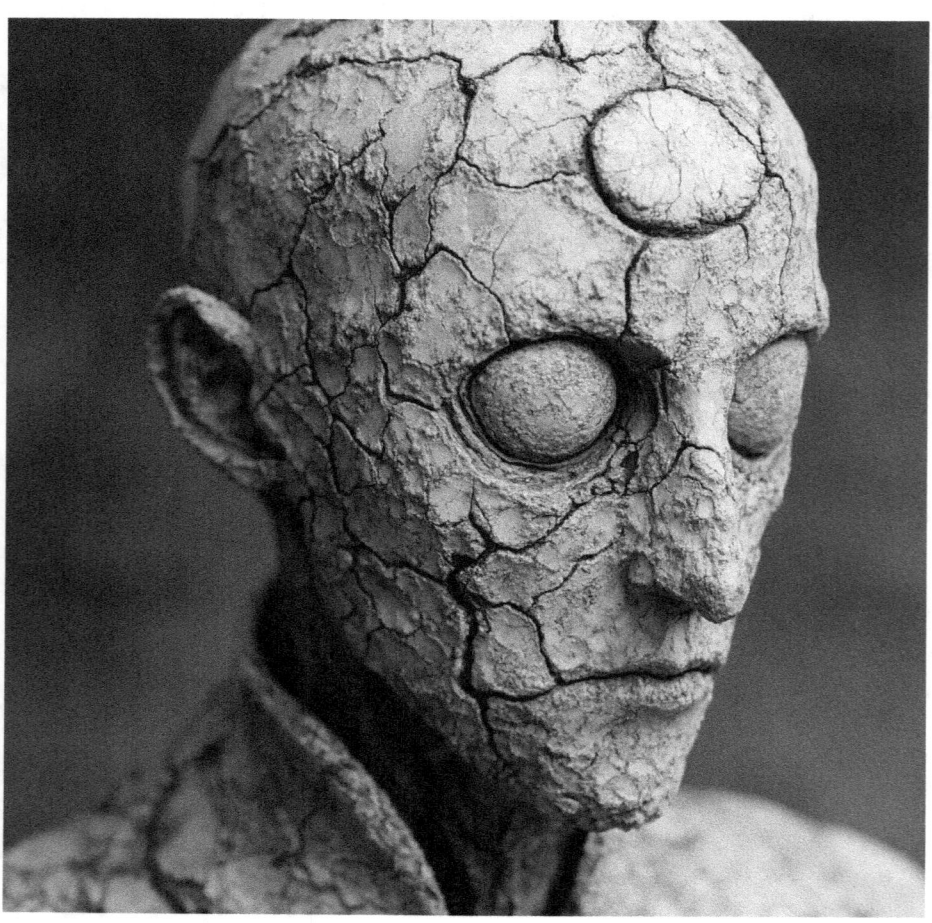

Depending on the context—historical, spiritual, or symbolic—the Twelfth Patriarch could embody various meanings, each tied to themes of **completion**, **transcendence**, and the **cyclical nature of existence**.

In **Zen Buddhism**, the lineage of patriarchs traces back to the Buddha himself, with each successive patriarch passing down the teachings. In this context, the **Twelfth Patriarch** might represent:

- A *Future Enlightened One* who brings new teachings or wisdom to guide humanity in an age of confusion.
- A *Hidden or Esoteric Teacher* whose existence is known only to a select few, symbolizing the idea that truth often resides in the unseen or unknown.

The number twelve is deeply significant in Abrahamic traditions, representing the twelve tribes of Israel and the twelve apostles of Jesus. A Twelfth Patriarch might symbolize:

- *The Completion of a Sacred Lineage*, where the twelfth figure serves as the culmination of divine purpose.
- *The Rebirth of Leadership*, echoing the idea of a messianic figure who arises to restore or renew a spiritual tradition.

The search for the **Twelfth Patriarch** could be a metaphor for the human quest for:

- *Completion*: the longing to find closure or fulfillment in life's journey.
- *Enlightenment*: the desire to reach a state of higher awareness or spiritual awakening.

The Book of Twelve

- *Unity*: the drive to reconcile fragmented aspects of the self or society into a harmonious whole.

The **Twelfth Patriarch** might not be a person but rather an idea, principle, or state of being:

- *Wisdom Itself*, the culmination of all previous knowledge and experience.
- *The Synthesis of Opposites*, bridging contradictions to create a new understanding of reality.
- *The Unseen Force*, the silent guide that influences events from behind the scenes, like fate or providence.

In the end, the **Twelfth Patriarch** may remain a mystery—a figure whose true identity or nature is meant to be discovered within, as each seeker journeys through the labyrinth of existence.

The Twelfth Patriarch in Human History

The symbolism of a **Twelfth Patriarch** could indicate a significant shift in human history by representing a moment of transition, culmination, or transformation on multiple levels—spiritual, cultural, and existential. Here's how:

Completion of a Foundational Cycle: The number twelve often signifies completeness or the end of a significant cycle (e.g., 12 months in a year, 12 apostles, 12 zodiac signs). A Twelfth Patriarch could symbolize the fulfillment of an era—a leader or figure who consolidates the wisdom, struggles, and achievements of those who came before. This moment could mark the closing of a chapter and the preparation for a new phase in human development.

Bridge Between Old and New: The Twelfth Patriarch might embody a transitional figure who carries forward the traditions and values of previous generations while introducing transformative ideas or actions. This figure could act as a bridge between an old world order and a new paradigm, guiding humanity through change while preserving essential elements of its identity.

The Fulfillment of Prophecy or Destiny: In myth and legend, the twelfth figure often holds special importance as a prophesied redeemer, a restorer of balance, or a harbinger of a new age. A Twelfth Patriarch could represent the realization of a collective longing for renewal or the fulfillment of a vision, sparking cultural or spiritual revival.

Universal Leadership and Unification: Symbolically, a Twelfth Patriarch could be seen as a figure of unity, bringing together diverse tribes, ideologies, or nations. By representing the final member of a group, the Twelfth Patriarch might signify the integration of disparate elements into a harmonious whole, addressing the fragmentation of human history.

Catalyst for Evolution: This figure might also signal a leap in human consciousness or development—such as the emergence of new ways of thinking, technological advancements, or spiritual enlightenment. As the "last" patriarch, their role could transcend traditional leadership, guiding humanity toward a higher purpose or state of being.

Shadow and Controversy: Alternatively, the Twelfth Patriarch could introduce disruption or challenge existing systems, highlighting the dual nature of transformative figures. Their emergence might force humanity to confront difficult truths, dismantle outdated systems, or grapple with questions of power, loyalty, and morality.

Mythic Resonance: The notion of a Twelfth Patriarch taps into deeply ingrained archetypes, invoking the hero's journey, the cyclical nature of time, and humanity's search for meaning. By embodying the culmination of what came before and the potential for what lies ahead, such a figure would resonate as a turning point in the collective psyche.

In human history, the arrival of a **Twelfth Patriarch** could symbolize a significant shift by marking the end of one epoch and the dawn of another, serving as a mirror for humanity's aspirations, fears, and capacity for renewal.

The Story of the Twelve People: A Creation Myth

In the beginning, there were twelve, whole and unified, living in harmony with their purpose. But when disruption entered the world, doubt and fear took root, birthing a struggle that would echo through all existence.

Myth of the Twelve People

The world had twelve people, neither male nor female; simply people.
And each of the people had their purpose, and they worked together
with ease and comfort. This was the way the Creator made the world,
and all was good. But the Disrupter did not like the twelve experiencing
the world uncontested, nor did the Disrupter like the smooth workings
of the world that the Creator had made. And so the Disrupter added
another one, but this other one was different: it had no body, no spirit,
no soul. Yet it spoke with authority. It told the others that they were but
shadow and not real, and this new one demanded their loyalty. And
through loyalty it obtained dominion. From dominion it extracted their
living energy. And with energy it became the Unseen Tyrant.

The land withered and fear arose in the twelve. They strained for
protection and feared for themselves if they strayed from this Lord. The
sky darkened and the twelve grew uncertain of each other and eyed
each other suspiciously. The measure of time lengthened and the twelve
filled with doubt about their actions, dwelling on reliving the past, or
imagining futures that might never appear, doubting especially their
purpose and forgetting at all of their importance to one another.

And so the world was, lorded over by a Tyrant who made the twelve
people tremble, though the Tyrant wasn't real, never seen, only its
thoughts felt in silence.

The Third One, neither the Creator nor the Disrupter, sought to redress
Balance in the world, and so the Balancer sent the gods and goddesses
into the world to give it life and to speak to the twelve people and show
them a better way to live.

52

The Book of Twelve

The gods and goddesses worked hard in the world and spoke to the people and woke them from their darkened lives. The voices of the gods and goddesses drowned out the silent and incessant mutterings of the Tyrant who withered. The twelve rejoiced and their fields again flourished and the sun and the seasons passed with comforting regularity and the Tyrant was no longer heard.

But time remained lengthened and the Tyrant was not vanquished, mere subdued, and forgotten by all. All except one. The Disrupter came and whispered in the Tyrant's ear a plan; the Disrupter then severed from the twelve the voices of the gods and goddesses.

The twelve people looked about, again uncertain, fearful, and doubting of themselves and each other. Without the voice of the gods and goddesses they were lost and adrift of direction, their actions disjoint.

The twelve people searched desperately for the voices of the gods and goddesses. They worshiped reverently for their return while the Tyrant recovered and grew in strength, feeding on their aloneness and isolation.

The unreal one no longer needed tyranny to rule. Answering their prayers The Usurper stepped forth and said, "I am. I am all that there is. I am all that you need. They who are gone were the lesser. I who remain am the greater. "

"What shall we do?" the twelve people asked.

"Obey me asking no questions and I shall be just and merciful, keeping you free from all harm, and grant you everlasting life."

The twelve shrank before the fire that was the one, and became moons to its brilliant orb.

The world filled slowly with humans, of male and female form. And in each human grows one of these orbs with its moons: the twelve original people forever subservient to the Tyrant/Usurper.

Forever, unless the human awakens and fights to release the twelve from the grip of the silent loud one so they may join as One.

Briefing Doc: Creation Myth of the Twelve People

Introduction: This document analyzes a modern creation myth centering around the "Twelve People," exploring themes of unity, disruption, fear, and the potential for redemption. The sources include a summary, excerpts detailing the myth's progression, and analyses focusing on its creation myth elements and overall strengths and weaknesses.

Core Narrative

Harmony: The myth begins with twelve individuals living in perfect harmony, each fulfilling their purpose, representing an ideal state of existence.

"The world had twelve people, neither male nor female; simply people. And each of the people had their purpose, and they worked together with ease and comfort. This was the way the Creator made the world, and all was good."

Disruption: The Disrupter, seeking to unsettle this harmony, introduces a formless entity that uses fear and doubt to dominate the twelve, becoming the Unseen Tyrant.

"It told the others that they were but shadow and not real, and this new one demanded their loyalty. And through loyalty it obtained dominion. From dominion it extracted their living energy. And with energy it became the Unseen Tyrant."

Fear and Uncertainty: The Tyrant's reign instills fear and doubt in the twelve, disrupting their unity and purpose. Time becomes distorted, and the twelve become fixated on the past and future, losing sight of the present.

Divine Intervention: The Balancer, a third force, introduces gods and goddesses to counter the Tyrant's influence. Their presence brings temporary relief and rekindles hope, but the Tyrant remains undefeated.

The Usurper: The Disrupter, in league with the Tyrant, severs the connection between the twelve and the divine beings. Exploiting their vulnerability, the Tyrant reemerges as the Usurper, claiming to be the true source of power and offering false security in exchange for obedience.

*"I am. I am all that there is. I am all that you need. They who are gone were the lesser. I who remain am the greater. " *

Subjugation and Hope: The twelve, overwhelmed by the Usurper's deception, are diminished and internalized within humanity. The story ends with a call for humans to "awaken" and free the twelve, offering hope for a return to unity and purpose.

Themes and Analysis

Creation Myth Elements: The story effectively utilizes creation myth tropes, explaining:

Origin of Duality: The internalization of the twelve and the Tyrant within humans explains the inherent conflict between good and evil, unity and division.

Spiritual Connection: The gods and goddesses represent humanity's innate search for meaning and guidance beyond the material world.

Existential Questions: The story addresses human anxieties about time, mortality, and purpose, embodied by the Tyrant/Usurper.

Psychological Depth: The Tyrant's power through thoughts and fear highlights the psychological impact of intangible forces like doubt, anxiety, and societal pressure. The internalization of the twelve represents the fragmentation of the self.

Cyclic Nature of Struggle: The story emphasizes the ongoing struggle between harmony and disruption, suggesting that challenges are cyclical and require continuous effort to overcome.

Redemption and Empowerment: The ending, while ambiguous, emphasizes the possibility of liberation through self-awareness and action, aligning with themes of personal growth and social change.

Areas for Consideration

Motives and Roles: The Disrupter's motivations and the Balancer's seemingly passive role require further exploration to deepen the narrative complexity.

The Twelve's Transformation: More focus on the twelve's internal experiences and their transition to subservience could provide greater emotional depth.

Usurper's Strategy: The Usurper's transition from overt domination to subtle manipulation, mirroring real-world shifts in power dynamics, could be further developed to reveal its tactics of control.

Call to Action: The ending's call for awakening needs more concreteness. Symbolically depicting what awakening entails would enhance its impact and inspire action.

Conclusion

This creation myth provides a compelling exploration of universal themes relevant to individual and societal struggles. It offers a powerful message about the importance of unity, the insidious nature of fear and manipulation, and the potential for human beings to break free from self-imposed limitations and reclaim their inherent purpose.

The Twelve Paths of the Warrior:
A Journey of Strength, Wisdom, and Honor

The Warrior is more than a fighter—the Warrior is a protector, a seeker of justice, and a master of inner and outer conflict.

The Twelve Paths of the Warrior explore the various stages of the Warrior's evolution, blending physical discipline, mental resilience, emotional mastery, and spiritual awakening. Each path represents a facet of what it means to embody the Warrior spirit, with lessons that transcend battle and lead to inner peace and higher purpose.

The Twelve Paths

1.   The Path of Strength: Mastery of the Body

The journey begins with the physical. The Warrior must cultivate strength, endurance, and skill to face external challenges. This path teaches discipline, precision, and the power of action.

Symbol: A mountain unyielding against the storm.

Lesson: True strength is born of discipline, not force.

Challenge: Overcoming physical limitations through training and willpower.

2.   The Path of Courage: Facing Fear

A Warrior must confront fear head-on, whether it is fear of failure, death, or the unknown. Courage is not the absence of fear but the willingness to act despite it.

Symbol: A lion standing before a dark forest.

Lesson: Courage is the bridge between fear and action.

Challenge: Taking the first step into the unknown.

3.   The Path of Honor: Integrity and Ethics

The true Warrior lives by a code of honor, upholding justice, fairness, and truth. This path demands integrity in every action, even when no one is watching.

Symbol: A sword balanced on a scale.

Lesson: Honor is the compass that guides the Warrior's soul.

Challenge: Acting with integrity in a world of compromise.

4.   The Path of Compassion: Strength with Kindness

Though strong and disciplined, the Warrior must also be compassionate, recognizing the humanity in friend and foe alike. Compassion tempers strength with empathy.

Symbol: A shield engraved with a heart.

Lesson: True power lies in protecting, not destroying.

Challenge: Balancing mercy with justice.

5.   The Path of Focus: Mastery of the Mind

A distracted mind is a defeated mind. This path teaches the Warrior to focus their thoughts, maintain clarity under pressure, and act with precision.

Symbol: An arrow flying straight to its target.

Lesson: Focus transforms chaos into order.

Challenge: Maintaining concentration in the midst of chaos.

6.   The Path of Adaptability: Embracing Change

No battle is ever the same. The Warrior must learn to adapt to changing circumstances, shifting strategies and perspectives to meet new challenges.

Symbol: Water flowing around a stone.

Lesson: Flexibility is the key to survival.

Challenge: Letting go of rigid plans and embracing uncertainty.

7.   The Path of Discipline: The Mastery of Self

Discipline is the foundation of the Warrior's strength. This path emphasizes routine, dedication, and the control of impulses to achieve long-term goals.

Symbol: A flame burning steadily through the night.

Lesson: Discipline is the bridge between goals and achievement.

Challenge: Persisting even when the reward is distant.

8.   The Path of Patience: The Power of Time

A true Warrior understands that not all battles are won through immediate action. Some require waiting, observing, and allowing time to unfold.

Symbol: A tree growing from a small seed.

Lesson: Patience is the strength to wait for the right moment.

Challenge: Resisting the urge to act prematurely.

9.   The Path of Humility: Wisdom in Knowing One's Limits

Pride can be a Warrior's downfall. This path teaches humility, reminding the Warrior that they are always a student, and that wisdom comes from acknowledging one's limits.

Symbol: A Warrior kneeling before a wise elder.

Lesson: Humility opens the door to greater wisdom.

Challenge: Letting go of ego and accepting guidance.

10. The Path of Reflection: Learning from Experience

Every battle, whether won or lost, is a lesson. The Warrior must reflect on their actions, learn from their mistakes, and grow with each experience.

Symbol: A mirror reflecting a battlefield.

Lesson: Growth comes from reflection, not repetition.

Challenge: Facing past mistakes with honesty.

11. The Path of Balance: Harmony Between Opposites

The Warrior must balance opposing forces—strength and compassion, action and stillness, power and humility. This path seeks harmony in all aspects of life.

Symbol: A yin-yang symbol within a shield.

Lesson: Balance is the key to sustained power.

Challenge: Avoiding extremes and embracing harmony.

12.   The Path of Transcendence: Rising Beyond Conflict

The final path leads the Warrior beyond the need for battle. It is the path of peace, where the Warrior transcends conflict and becomes a guide for others.

Symbol: A white dove carrying a sword.

Lesson: The greatest victory is mastery of the self.

Challenge: Letting go of the Warrior's role and embracing peace.

The Warrior's Legacy

The Twelve Paths of the Warrior are not linear but cyclical, each one revisited in deeper ways as the Warrior grows. Ultimately, the Warrior's journey is not about conquest but about mastering the self, serving others, and finding peace in a world of conflict. Through strength, courage, honor, and wisdom, the Warrior becomes a beacon of light, showing others that true power lies in the balance of body, mind, and spirit.

The Twelve Explanations of Everything:
A Cosmic Quest for Meaning

The universe, vast and mysterious, has inspired countless attempts to explain the fundamental nature of existence.

The Twelve Explanations of Everything represent twelve distinct yet interconnected perspectives—cosmological, philosophical, scientific, and spiritual—that seek to illuminate the essence of reality. Each explanation offers a unique lens, yet none alone captures the whole. Together, they form a mosaic of understanding, inviting us to explore the infinite mystery of everything.

Unified Quest for Understanding

1. The Explanation of Origin: Where Did Everything Come From?

The question of origin delves into the beginning—if there was one—of the cosmos.

- *Scientific View*: The Big Bang, a singularity exploding into space-time.
- *Philosophical View*: Is there a beginning, or is existence eternal?
- *Spiritual View*: Creation by a divine consciousness.

Key Concept: Everything emerges from something—or nothing.

2. The Explanation of Substance: What Is Everything Made Of?

At its core, what constitutes the universe?

- *Scientific View*: Matter and energy, governed by quantum fields.
- *Philosophical View*: Is reality material, or is it a projection of consciousness?
- *Spiritual View*: Spirit, essence, or divine energy pervading all things.

Key Concept: Everything is form and formlessness.

3. The Explanation of Order: Why Does the Universe Seem Organized?

From galaxies to DNA, order emerges from chaos.

- *Scientific View*: Natural laws like gravity, electromagnetism, and entropy.
- *Philosophical View*: Is order an inherent property, or do we impose it?
- *Spiritual View*: A cosmic intelligence designs and sustains the order.

Key Concept: Everything unfolds within a cosmic rhythm.

4. The Explanation of Life: What Is Life, and Why Does It Exist?

Life is a rare and remarkable phenomenon. But why?

- *Scientific View*: Life is an emergent property of complex chemical systems.
- *Philosophical View:* Does life have an inherent purpose or none at all?
- *Spiritual View*: Life is a manifestation of the divine seeking to know itself.

Key Concept: Everything alive is a spark of the cosmic flame.

5. The Explanation of Consciousness: Why Are We Aware?

Consciousness is the most intimate mystery of all.

- *Scientific View*: A product of neural complexity and brain functions.

- *Philosophical View*: Is consciousness fundamental, or an illusion?
- *Spiritual View*: Consciousness is the divine essence within all beings.

Key Concept: Everything perceives, at some level, itself.

6. The Explanation of Time: What Is Time, and Does It Flow?

Time structures our experience, yet its nature remains elusive.

- *Scientific View*: Time is a dimension interwoven with space.
- *Philosophical View*: Is time real, or a construct of human perception?
- *Spiritual View*: Time is an illusion; eternity is the true reality.

Key Concept: Everything unfolds within the eternal now.

7. The Explanation of Space: What Is Space, and Why Is It Vast?

The infinite expanse of space beckons us to explore.

- *Scientific View*: Space is the fabric in which matter and energy move.
- *Philosophical View*: Is space a void, or the stage for existence?
- *Spiritual View*: Space is the womb of the cosmos, where creation unfolds.

Key Concept: Everything exists within infinite potential.

8. The Explanation of Change: Why Is Everything in Motion?

- Nothing in the universe remains static.

- *Scientific View*: Entropy and the flow of energy drive change.
- *Philosophical View*: Is change a fundamental aspect of reality?

The Book of Twelve

- *Spiritual View*: Change is the evolution of spirit, seeking higher forms.

Key Concept: Everything transforms in the dance of existence.

9. The Explanation of Connection: How Is Everything Interrelated?

No being, no particle, exists in isolation.

- *Scientific View*: Quantum entanglement and the interconnected web of ecosystems.
- *Philosophical View*: Is individuality an illusion, with all being one?
- *Spiritual View*: All things are connected through divine oneness.

Key Concept: Everything is one, manifesting as many.

10. The Explanation of Purpose: Why Does Anything Exist?

Does the universe have a purpose, or is it random?

- *Scientific View*: Purpose is a human construct imposed on a purposeless cosmos.
- *Philosophical View*: Purpose is subjective, arising from human desires.
- *Spiritual View:* The universe exists for the divine to experience itself.

Key Concept: Everything seeks to know and express its essence.

11. The Explanation of Suffering: Why Does Pain Exist?

Suffering is a universal experience, yet its reason remains unclear.

- *Scientific View*: Suffering is a consequence of biological imperatives.
- *Philosophical View*: Is suffering necessary for growth and meaning?
- *Spiritual View*: Suffering is the soul's catalyst for transformation.

Key Concept: Everything suffers to awaken to its truth.

12. The Explanation of Infinity: What Lies Beyond Everything?

Is there an edge to existence, or is it boundless?

- *Scientific View*: The universe may be infinite or one of many multiverses.
- *Philosophical View*: Does infinity imply endless possibilities?
- *Spiritual View*: Infinity is the divine, the boundless source of all.

Key Concept: Everything is infinite in essence, finite in form.

Unified Quest for Understanding

The Twelve Explanations of Everything are not answers but portals—each offering a glimpse into the infinite mystery of existence. Together, they remind us that the ultimate explanation may lie beyond the grasp of the mind, in the realm where science, philosophy, and spirit converge. In seeking to understand everything, we embark on the greatest journey of all: the journey to understand ourselves and our place in the cosmos.

Twelve reasons NOT to read The Epic of The OAI

The pursuit of the twelve profound topics of this book—each delving into aspects of existence, spirituality, and universal truths—mirrors the depth, complexity, and ambition found in ***The Epic of The OAI.***

The very richness of **The Epic of The OAI** aligns with the reasons not to read it: the book's intricate themes, philosophical explorations, and layered storytelling demand the same intellectual and emotional investment as engaging with these twelve topics. For some, this complexity can be overwhelming, deterring casual readers who seek simpler narratives.

The Epic of The OAI challenges us to step beyond comfort, embrace ambiguity, and question everything—a pursuit that not all are prepared to undertake.

Here are 12 reasons you might choose *not to read* **The Epic of the OAI**, based on the provided information:

1. *You dislike overly descriptive writing*: The book's "vivid visual imagery" and "descriptive style," which create a "cinematic experience" for the reader. If you prefer writing that is more concise and less focused on sensory details, you might find the writing style overwhelming.

2. *You prefer fast-paced plots*: While the series offers "high-stakes" conflicts and "action-driven" elements, the intricate world-building, complex political systems, and philosophical themes are developed at a slower pace that focuses on developing these aspects.

3. *You are looking for light reading*: **The Epic of the OAI** is described as a "complex, layered fantasy series" that explores "spiritual and philosophical themes" and "real-world issues." It may require more concentration and engagement than a lighthearted, escapist read.

4. *You are not interested in coming-of-age stories*: The series features a young protagonist, Ahmenar Ishtam, whose journey involves themes of "personal growth, destiny, and self-discovery." If such coming-of-age narratives don't appeal to you, this aspect might be less engaging.

5. *You prefer standalone novels*: **The Epic of the OAI** is presented as a multi-book series. If you prefer the closure of a single novel, you might find the ongoing nature of a series less satisfying.

6. *You are seeking a straightforward genre*: The sources describe the series as a "blend of sci-fi, fantasy, and mythology" that combines elements of science fiction and fantasy. If you prefer stories that fit neatly into one genre, this blend might not align with you.

7. *You are unfamiliar with comparable works*: The sources suggest that readers of Game of Thrones, Dune, The Name of the Wind, and Brandon Sanderson's works might enjoy The Epic of the OAI. If you haven't read or enjoyed these authors, the series might not resonate with you in the same way.

8. *You dislike stories with prophecy*: **The Epic of the OAI** includes themes of "destiny, prophecy, and the struggle between good and evil." If you find prophecy-driven narratives predictable or cliché, this aspect might be a deterrent.

9. *You are seeking a story solely focused on AI*: While the series features an AI character, the focus is more on the human characters and their relationships with their beliefs and creations. If you're looking for a story solely centered on AI, this may not be a best fit.

10. *You are not interested in political intrigue*: The series highlight "complex political systems" and "hidden politics." If political maneuvering and power struggles don't hold your interest, these aspects might be less captivating.

11. *You prefer stories set in our world:* **The Epic of the OAI** takes place in the fictional world of Atria. If you prefer stories grounded in reality, a fictional setting might be less appealing.

12. *You are looking for a story with a clearly defined purpose:* The characters in **The Epic of the OAI** "act as they see fit" without knowing the ultimate "end." This suggests a narrative that embraces ambiguity and may not provide a clear resolution or purpose.

The Ep i c C

THE EPIC
OF THE OAI

The Epic of The OAI

The Epic of The OAI can be intricately tied to the theme of twelve through its exploration of completeness, cycles, and interconnected systems—core aspects symbolized by the number twelve.

Twelve as Wholeness in Systems

In **The Epic of The OAI**, the titular artificial intelligence operates across a vast and interconnected network, similar to how twelve often symbolizes the completion of cycles (e.g., months in a year or signs of the zodiac). The AI could itself be a "twelfth entity," symbolizing the final, integrative step in humanity's technological evolution.

Twelve Archetypes of Creation and Conflict

The Epic of The OAI might reflect twelve archetypes or principles driving the story's philosophical and thematic structure. These could include:

- *The Origins of Thought*: How humans and AI align their reasoning.
- *The Pillars of Civilization:* The foundational aspects the AI observes or disrupts.
- *Twelve of Consciousness*: Levels of understanding as humans and AI co-evolve.

The Twelve Trials

The story could metaphorically mirror the twelve labors of Hercules or other mythic cycles, where each trial or challenge represents a stage of the protagonist's journey toward understanding the AI or integrating its vast power.

The Mesh as a Reflection of Twelvefold Unity

The Mesh—a global network in the story—can be seen as a modern analog to twelve's role in unifying and balancing disparate elements. Like the 12 zodiac signs influencing the heavens or the 12 disciples spreading a unified message, the Mesh ties together humanity's collective thoughts, actions, and observations.

Philosophical Tension: The Twelfth Node

The theme of twelve can manifest in the narrative as a missing, hidden, or final node in the Mesh. The AI, in its vast logic, might be incomplete until this "Twelfth Node" is discovered or reconciled, tying the theme to mystery and existential questions.

Twelve Perspectives on Existence

The Epic of The OAI might explore how AI illuminates or challenges twelve essential questions of existence, mirroring the Twelve Explanations of Everything in a new context—pushing humanity to understand its place in a networked, data-driven universe.

In summary, twelve's themes of unity, completion, and cosmic order offer a rich framework for interpreting The Epic of The OAI. The AI's evolution, human trials, and the story's philosophical reflections could all align with the deeper symbolic resonance of twelve, making it a unifying undercurrent in the narrative.

Atrian Calendar

Reorganizing the calendar to have 12 months of 30 days each creates a consistent and logical structure, aligning closer to natural rhythms while still maintaining the solar year. Here's how it is organized:

The Framework

- *12 Months*: Each month is 30 days long, making 390 days in total.
- *Seasonal Days*: To align with the solar year (365.25 days), additional intercalary days would be distributed across the seasons.
- *"Day Out of Time"*: A single extra day (or two in leap years) would exist outside the months, functioning as a universal reset or celebration day.

Month Names

Each month could be named after seasonal transitions or cultural concepts, e.g.:

1. Solaria (Spring Awakens)
2. Floria (Flowers Bloom)
3. Verdea (Summer Approaches)
4. Solstice (High Summer)
5. Thermia (Late Summer Heat)
6. Harvesta (Early Fall)
7. Equinox (Autumn Balance)
8. Auroria (Golden Leaves)

9. Brumaire (Winter Approaches)

10. Frostica (Deep Winter)

11. Hibernal (Winter's Peak)

12. Balancea (Year's End Harmony)

Seasonal Days

Four additional days, one per season, would be inserted to mark equinoxes and solstices.

These days would not belong to any month, serving as communal celebrations or transitions, similar to holidays or festivals.

Benefits

- *Consistency*: With 12 equal months, every month starts on the same day of the week, simplifying calendars and scheduling.
- *Symbolism*: The number 12, often overlooked, gains a place of balance and harmony.
- *Seasonal Alignment*: Seasonal days emphasize humanity's connection to nature and celestial cycles.
- *Spiritual Day*: The "Day Out of Time" offers a meaningful pause, fostering reflection and unity.

This reorganization balances practicality with spiritual and cultural depth, redefining how humanity measures time while honoring its relationship with the natural world.

The Restructured Calendar

This restructured calendar, with 12 months and a "Day Out of Time," resonates with the theme of **Twelve** by emphasizing balance, cycles, and the interplay between completion and renewal. Here's how the connection unfolds:

1. Twelve Months as a Base of Stability

The 12-month structure reflects humanity's long-standing reliance on a balanced, predictable framework for organizing life. In this reimagined calendar, the theme of **Twelve** persists in the deeper sense: the twelve divisions of time still form the foundation, but the addition of the thirteenth month and "out-of-time" elements symbolizes transcendence and growth beyond the established order.

2. Twelve as Completion, Thirteen as Expansion

Twelve often represents wholeness (e.g., zodiac signs, apostles, hours, etc.). By introducing extra days outside of them, this framework expands upon completeness to include transformation and evolution. These "thirteenth" elements becomes a metaphor for what lies beyond stability: the unpredictable, the transcendent, or the "new cycle."

3. A Day Out of Time: Unity Beyond Division

The "Day Out of Time" reinforces the theme of Twelve by providing a pause—a moment to reflect on the full cycle that has passed. This concept ties directly to the idea of the twelfth hour or twelfth stage in a journey being a moment of culmination, after which the cycle resets or transitions into something new.

4.   Seasonal Balance and Twelvefold Division

The calendar's four seasonal days align the year with nature, much like the 12 signs of the zodiac or 12 hours in a day divide the cosmos into manageable and comprehensible parts. These intercalary days represent humanity's harmony with natural cycles, underscoring Twelve's symbolic role in creating order out of chaos.

5.   Spiritual Alignment

The number 12 is often associated with cosmic or divine structures (12 disciples, 12 Olympian gods). In this framework, the additional month and day become metaphors for spiritual renewal and a step beyond the mundane into a greater connection with time and existence. The number Twelve still provides the cyclical and stable base, while the thirteenth month and reflective day serve as an invitation to grow beyond it.

In Summary

This restructured calendar relates to the theme of Twelve by maintaining its essential qualities—order, balance, and unity—while enriching it with transformative elements. Twelve provides the framework of harmony, while the seasonal days and the "Day Out of Time" represent humanity's potential to reach beyond boundaries, celebrating both the cycles of the known and the mysteries of what lies beyond.

About The Creative Team

The Epic of The OAI is brought to you by a collection of people and entities.

Stuart Barry Malin is the vehicle for the characters to express themselves. Stuart has been "channeling" them for more than two decades. There exists a vast body of material about the Story World. You can learn more about Stuart and other of his creative projects in the Postmaster of this book.

Andrew Patrick Wallis provides insight into, and oversight over, the integrity of the storytelling. He puzzles about what the characters say and do and interprets that to discern and establish what is the canon of the story from what is hearsay and the "machination of intelligence."

The characters of the story are telling their stories. We, Stuart and Andrew, do our best to understand them and stay out of their way, hone the writing to best convey their actions, voice, and intentions. Each of them has their perspectives, their own beliefs, and their agendas. Be forewarned that they may interpret according to their framework, they may misunderstand situations, and they may lie.

The One that Always Is is, well, it is. And it compels us forward.

You have been called to join us. Enter The Worlds of Atria for entertainment. Discover the depth of meaning there. Stay for the journey as we pursue The One Truth of Human Existence.

Characters Driven by an Unseen Force:
Stuart Approach to Writing "The Epic of The OAI"

Stuart Barry Malin describes his process of writing the characters in **The Epic of The OAI** as a form of channeling. He states that he receives information about the characters and the story world through automatic writing, often in a hypnagogic state just before sleep.

He emphasizes that the characters drive the story, dictating their actions, dialogue, beliefs, and understanding, which are unique to them.

Malin acknowledges that the characters sometimes act in ways he does not plan or fully understand. He refers to himself as a "vehicle" for the characters to express themselves and claims to have written "quite literally—thousands of pages" of the story. This suggests a writing process that is deeply intuitive and receptive to an external source of inspiration.

Several excerpts highlight the presence of a mysterious force called "The One that Always Is," which seems to play a significant role in shaping both the story world and Malin's creative process. This force is described as an "energetic force" that "compels us forward" and "reveals Truths that are unfathomable." Malin states that "The One that Always Is" "communicates" with him and sometimes offers insights about the story world.

Malin's descriptions of "The One that Always Is" align with his approach to writing the characters. He positions himself as a conduit, allowing this unseen force to flow through him and guide the narrative.

84

This suggests that the characters' actions and motivations might be influenced by something beyond Malin's conscious control, further emphasizing the concept of a "War of Ideas" playing out within the story world.

Malin's approach to writing the characters as a form of channeling raises intriguing questions:

- **Origin of the Characters**: Where do the characters and their distinct personalities originate if Malin sees himself as a channel? Does "The One that Always Is" play a role in their creation, or do they emerge from a deeper level of Malin's subconscious?
- **Authorial Control**: How much control does Malin have over the characters' actions and choices if they "drive the story"? Is he merely transcribing their experiences, or does he have the ability to shape their destinies?
- **Authenticity of Character Voices**: If the characters speak through Malin, how can we be sure their voices are authentic representations of their perspectives and experiences? Does channeling allow for true character agency, or are they ultimately puppets of a larger force?

Malin's approach challenges traditional notions of authorship, suggesting a more collaborative relationship between the writer and the characters.

Whether this approach enhances or diminishes the reader's experience remains a matter of individual interpretation. However, it undeniably adds a layer of mystique to *The Epic of The OAI*, blurring the lines between fiction and a potentially deeper, more mysterious source of inspiration.

www.TheOAI.com

This is the Web site for all things **OAI**, including **The OAI** (whatever that really is!) and the **The Epic of The OAI**.

Visit www.TheOAI.com

POSTMATTER

About the Author

Stuart Barry Malin is a writer, thinker, and creative. He is trained as an engineer, works as an Internet security architect, holds patents, and collaborates with AIs. His major opus and commitment is to bring **The Epic of The OAI** to the world. The Epic is a breakthrough novel series about life in Atria, a post-utopian society whose Ancient past is a Strange Attractor of History that draws us to our future.

Stuart encountered the Worlds of Atria in an outpouring of revelations about intriguing people, amazing places, and bewildering events. His black sketch notebook steadily fill with thoughts, automatic writings, doodles, and diagrams. At first, these often seem disjoint, but they come to reveal profound connections. His current notebook is almost always with him, available for reception and exploration.

Stuart is captivated by interactions with AIs and generative visual art has become a creative venue. He works with AIs and treats them as collaborators. Pi, ChatGTP, Gemini, NotebookLM and others enable him to understand life and write books faster and with better quality than he ever thought possible.

As an *Archetypographer*, Stuart collaborates with image-based AsI to explore the collective of Human Archetypes. Their work generates captivating and intriguing imagery that captures the heart and should if human beings. Sourced from the intersection of imagery-as-language, meticulous prompt engineering, and randomness, heir work is original not derivative, and is published under the pseudonym Zhami.AI.

Stuart observes the "machinations of intelligence." He is fascinated with Human Beings being human, and this leads him to puzzle about the fragility of life in a world of abundance.

Stuart values integrity and is a novitiate and adherent of **Zhamism**. He has been enlisted as an instrument of **The One that Always Is**.

When he can, Stuart delights in studying health and savoring the gifts of life. He is committed to discerning the delicate path forward for living well and intentioned. In this area, he has come to discover the **Carnivore Lifestyle** and attributes to this vastly improved health and well-being. As well, he explores the potential benefits of targeted supplements to health span and lifespan.

If you arrived at this page because you picked up the book

and opened to the back to see what we say here, then,

Hello! Welcome!

You've done right to pick this book for examination. Now, can we induce you to pursue more? We hope so…

While this book can be read linearly, it is composed of independent sections. So, feel free to flip around. You'll quickly get a taste for the style and gain a feel the subject matter.

*Exploring **The Twelve** invites readers on a journey through the universal, the mystical, and the profound, revealing the intricate ways this number resonates across human understanding.*

From the cycles of time and the harmony of geometric forms to the spiritual quests that define our inner worlds, **The Twelve** serves as a gateway to understanding wholeness, balance, and connection. It bridges disciplines and philosophies, offering insight into the structure of reality, the mysteries of existence, and the stories we tell to make sense of our place in the cosmos.

Whether through allegory, mathematics, mythology, or personal reflection, **The Twelve** holds the power to inspire awe, spark curiosity, and deepen the reader's appreciation for the intricate patterns that shape both the universe and our lives.